Mr. Zinger's Hat
Cary Fagan Illustrated by Dušan Petričić

TUNDRA BOOKS

Published by Tundra Books, a division of Random House of Canada Limited

Published in Canada by Tundra Books,
75 Sherbourne Street, Toronto, Ontario M5A 2P9

Published in the United States by Tundra Books of Northern New York,
P.O. Box 1030, Plattsburgh, New York 12901

Library of Congress Control Number: 2011938764

Library and Archives Canada Cataloguing in Publication

Fagan, Cary
Mr. Zinger's hat / by Cary Fagan ; illustrated by Dušan Petričić
ISBN 978-1-77049-253-0
I. Petričić, Dušan II. Title.
PS8561.A375M59 2012 jC813'.54 C2011-906506-1

We acknowledge the financial support of the Government of Canada through the Canada Book Fund and that of the Government of Ontario through the Ontario Media Development Corporation's Ontario Book Initiative. We further acknowledge the support of the Canada Council for the Arts and the Ontario Arts Council for our publishing program.

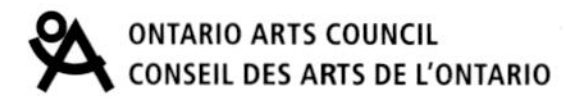

The illustrations in this book were rendered in watercolor.

Design: Jennifer Lum
Printed and bound in China

1 2 3 4 5 6 17 16 15 14 13 12

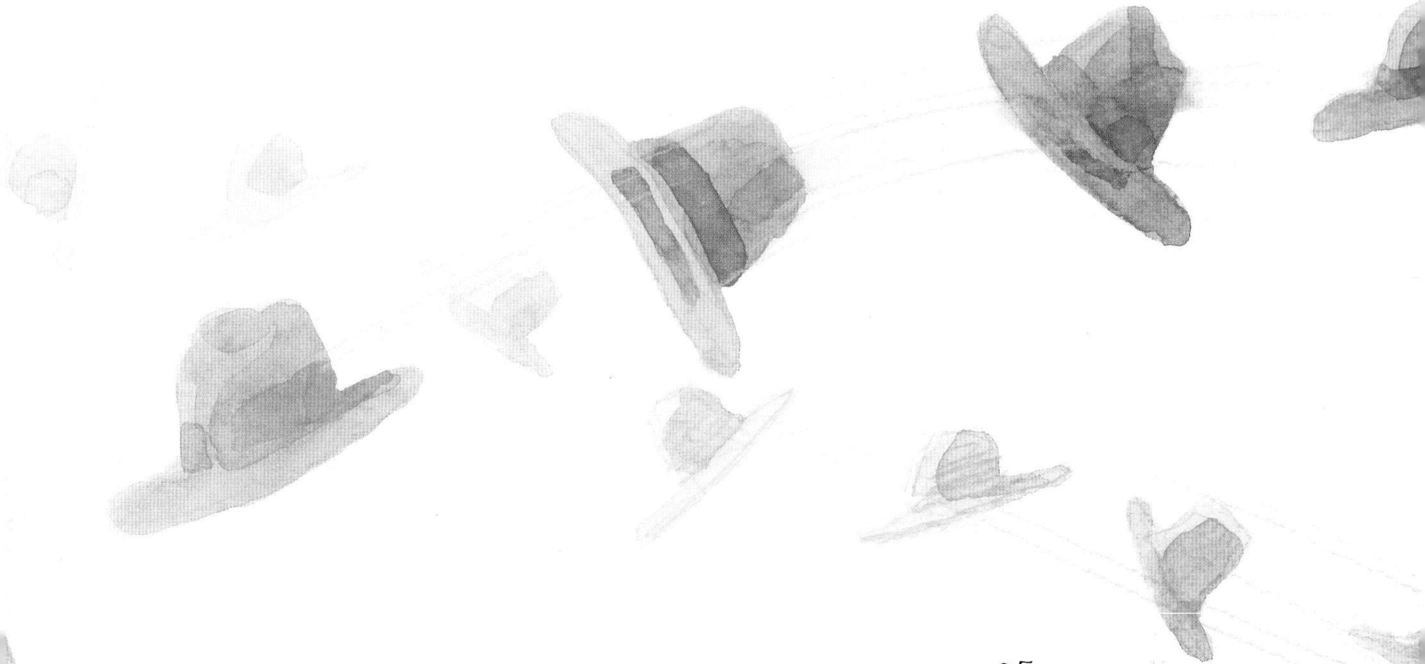

For David Diamond, who's good at listening and telling. –C.F.

For Bogdan Krsic, my late professor, with deep gratitude. –D.P.

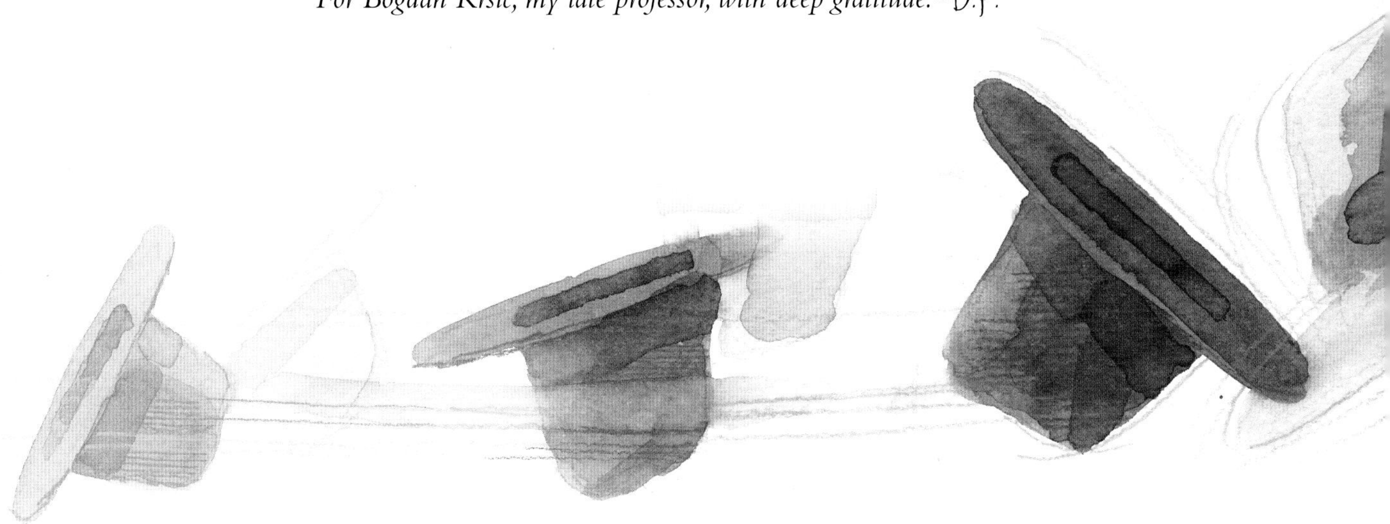

Every day after school, Leo took his ball into the courtyard. He threw the ball high into the air. It would hit the brick wall and bounce back, and Leo would try to catch it.

And every day, Leo saw Mr. Zinger. Mr. Zinger walked around the courtyard, over and over. He was small and old and, to Leo, looked like an elf or a goblin. He always wore a black suit and hat. He shuffled forward, deep in thought.

Mr. Zinger made up stories. The stories were published in magazines and in books, too. Leo's mother would say to him, "Don't disturb Mr. Zinger. He's making up stories. He's working."

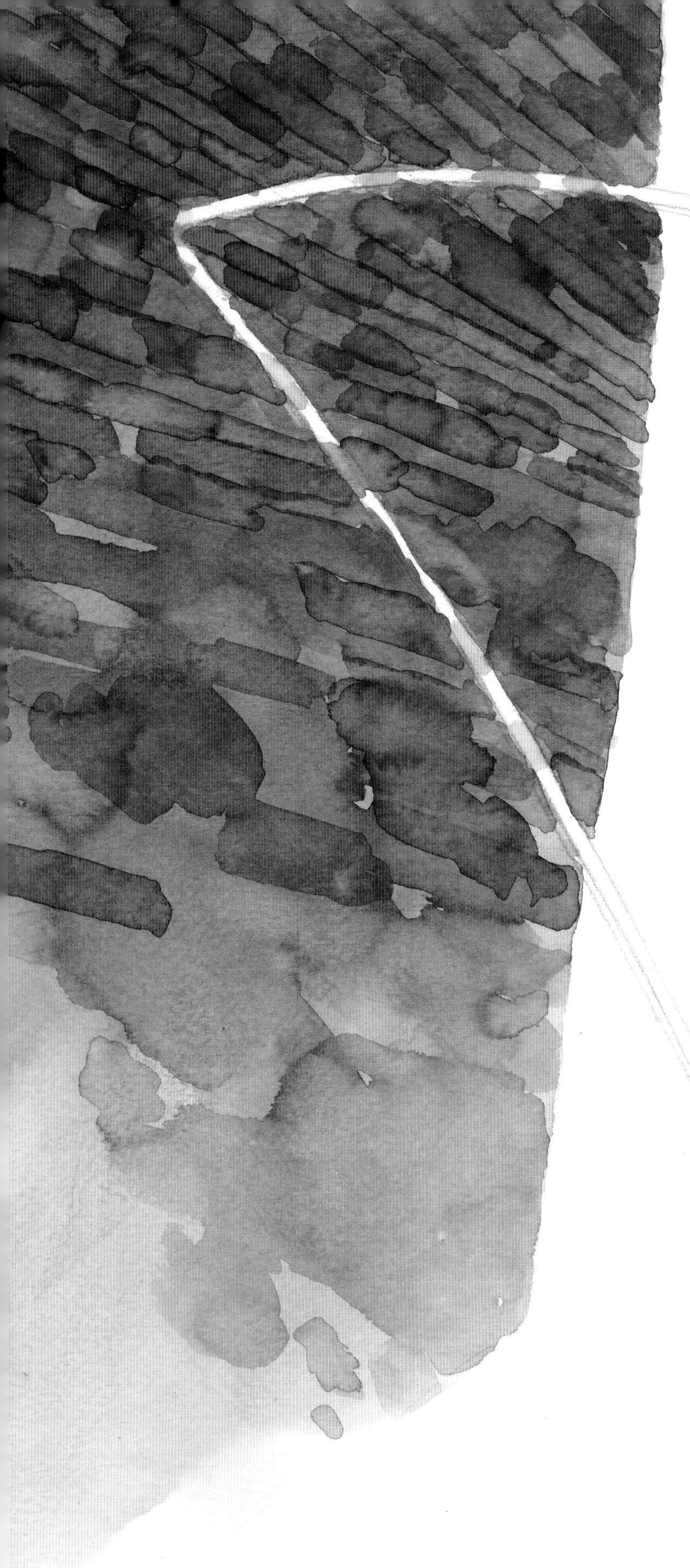

One afternoon Leo threw his ball higher than ever before. Up it went, until finally it smacked against the wall.

The ball bounced back and zipped across the courtyard – right toward Mr. Zinger!

Mr. Zinger didn't even notice. He was too busy thinking. *Biff!* The ball knocked Mr. Zinger's hat off his head.

"Oy, my hat!" cried Mr. Zinger. He reached up, but the wind had caught the hat and blown it high above the courtyard. Mr. Zinger patted his bald head.

"Young man!" he called. "Help me get my hat!"

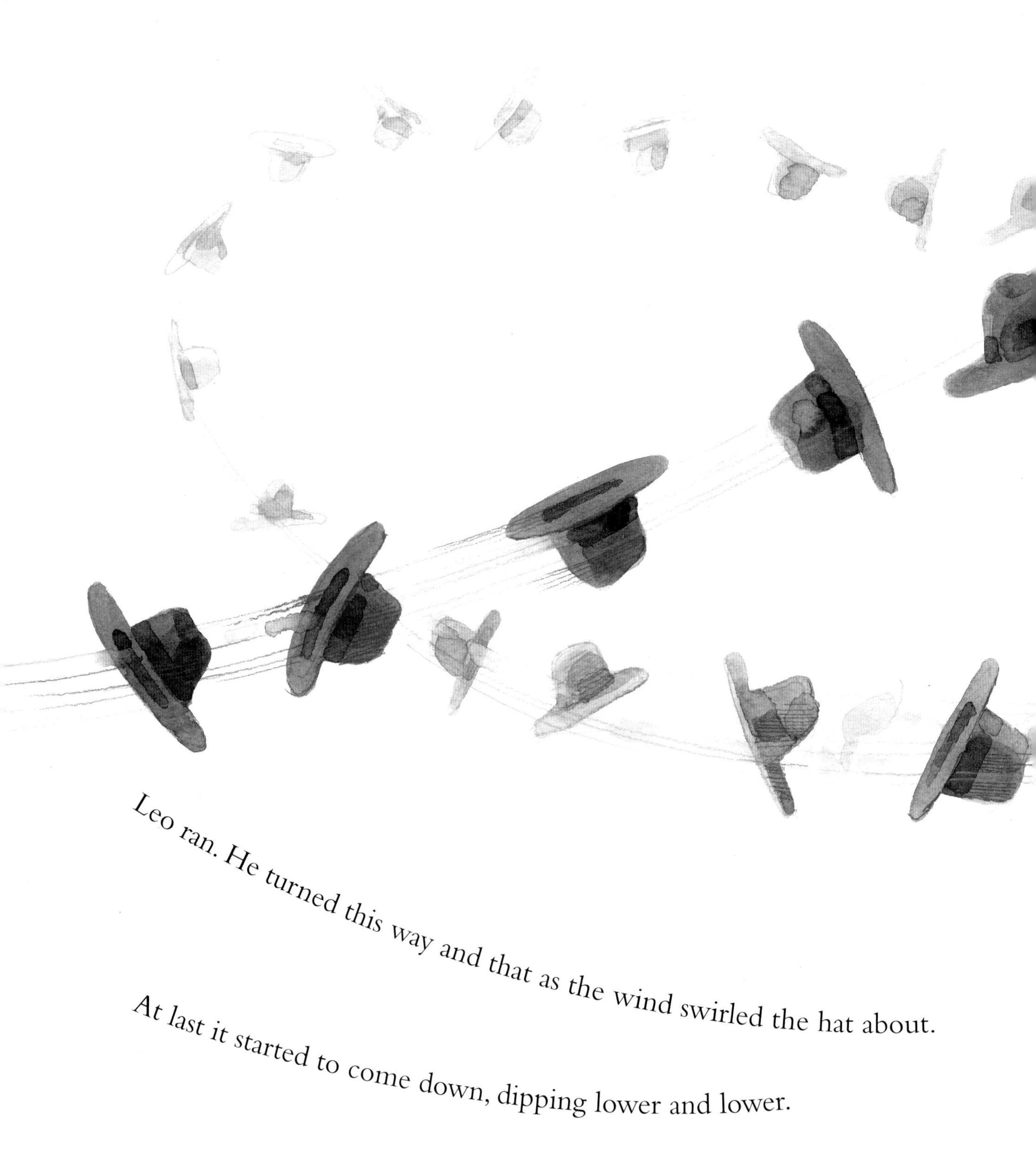

Leo ran. He turned this way and that as the wind swirled the hat about.

At last it started to come down, dipping lower and lower.

Leo held out his hands.

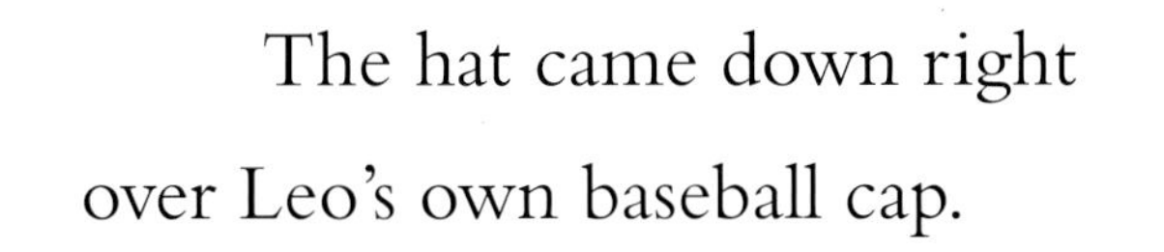

The hat came down right
over Leo's own baseball cap.

Leo took off the hat and gave it to Mr. Zinger.

"So much excitement," Mr. Zinger said. "It makes me tired. Come, young man. Let's sit on the bench."

So Leo sat on the bench beside Mr. Zinger.

"What is your name, young man?"

"Leo."

"Well, Leo, I wonder why my hat took off like that. Maybe there is something inside it." Mr. Zinger peered into the hat.

"What is it? What's inside the hat?" asked Leo. He looked, too, but he didn't see anything.

"Ah, I see now," said Mr. Zinger. "It's a story. A story trying to get out."

"What story?" asked Leo.

"Let me see," Mr. Zinger said, peering into the hat with his pale eyes. "Once upon a time, there was a man."

"Could it maybe be a boy?" asked Leo.

"Yes, you're right – a boy. Now this boy was very poor."

"He might be rich," Leo ventured.

Mr. Zinger scratched his head. "Why not? He was rich. Rich as a king, an emperor, a czar. He was also very unhappy. Can you see why?"

Leo looked into the hat. He thought a moment. "Because he had nothing to do?"

"Okay. So, one day, this boy makes a proclamation."

"What's a proclamation?" asked Leo.

"An announcement. He will give half of his wealth and possessions to any child who can cheer him up. Children from all over the land line up at the front door of the boy's mansion, hoping to be the one."

"This ought to be good," said Leo.

"The first child," said Mr. Zinger, "offered the boy a gold watch."

"Boring," said Leo.

"The boy thought so, too. The next child brought him –"

"An electric guitar?"

"Yes! But the boy already had a better one. And the other children brought him many more things."

"A diamond? A flat-screen TV? A canoe? A live monkey?"

"Yes, yes, yes, and again, yes. But either the boy already had those or else they didn't interest him. He was very disappointed. But just as he was closing the door of his mansion, he saw something."

Leo looked into the hat. "A boy. Running toward the door."

"Exactly," said Mr. Zinger.

"Did the boy running toward the door have a name?" asked Leo.

"Of course! Everybody has a name, doesn't he? But I can't quite make it out. Maybe you can."

It was dark inside the hat. Leo cocked his ear and listened. "Leo. The boy's name was Leo."

"As good a name as any," said Mr. Zinger. "So Leo went to the door all out of breath. The rich boy said to him, 'What have you got that all the others don't have?' And Leo held something up."

"What was it? What did he hold up?" asked Leo.

"You tell me," said Mr. Zinger.

"But I don't know," said Leo.

"You don't know? Are you so sure about that? You knew that the story was about a boy and not a man. You knew that he was rich and not poor. You knew that he didn't want a gold watch. You even knew the name of the boy who ran up to the door. So maybe you do know what *this* Leo held up. So? What was it?"

Leo thought. He closed his eyes and thought hard. At last he opened his eyes again.

"A ball."

"A ball?" said Mr. Zinger. "An ordinary ball . . . like your own ball?"

"Yes," said Leo.

"Okay, then," said Mr. Zinger. "So Leo held up an ordinary ball, and he said to the rich boy, 'Would you like to play catch with me?'"

"I know what the boy said," Leo told him. "He said yes."

"They played all afternoon, and the next day, too, and became best friends," said Mr. Zinger.

"And Leo didn't even want half of the boy's wealth," said Leo. "He gave it all away."

"Hmm. He's some boy, this Leo."

"Except for the electric guitar and the monkey. He kept those."

"And that's the end?" asked Mr. Zinger.

"Yes, that's the end."

"I like it."

"I like it, too."

Mr. Zinger got up with a groan. "And now, young man, I must return to my desk. I have a story to write."

"About Leo and the rich boy?"

Mr. Zinger put his hat back on his head. "No," he said. "That's not my story, that's your story. But maybe another story will try to get out of my hat. There's no end of them, you know."

Mr. Zinger smiled and nodded and walked slowly away.

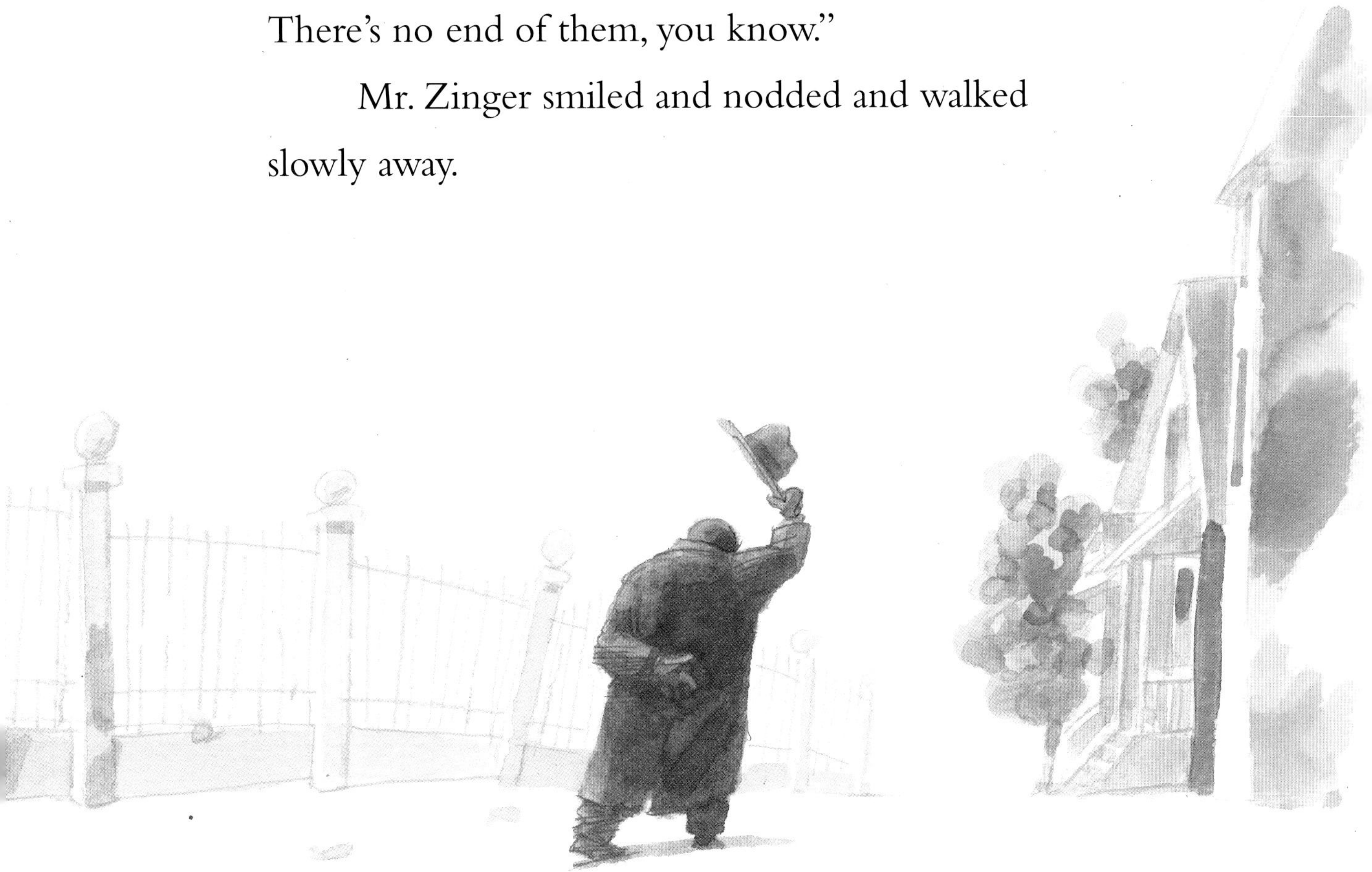

Leo looked at his ball. He threw the ball against the wall and caught it. He did it again . . . and again. He threw it once more, and this time it went very high, hit the wall, and bounced over Leo's head.

"I've got it!" somebody said. Leo turned. A girl. She caught the ball.

The girl came up to him. "Do you want to play catch?" she said.

For a long time they played catch. Then tag. Then hide-and-seek. Finally, they were too tired to play anything and sat on the bench.

“What’s your name?” Leo asked.

“Sophie.”

“Mine’s Leo.”

“Do you want to share my chocolate?” asked Sophie, taking a bar from her pocket.

“Sure.”

They sat eating the chocolate. Leo took off his baseball cap. He said, "I have a story inside my cap."

"I like stories."

"Once upon a time, there was a boy."

Sophie looked into the hat. "Can it be a girl?" she asked.

"Okay. A girl. She was rich as a queen, but she wasn't very happy. Do you know why?"

"Because her mother and father had been captured by an ogre?"

"Exactly," said Leo.